Questions & Answers
OCEANS

First published in 2016 by Miles Kelly Publishing Ltd
Harding's Barn, Bardfield End Green, Thaxted, Essex, CM6 3PX, UK

2 4 6 8 10 9 7 5 3 1

Publishing Director Belinda Gallagher
Creative Director Jo Cowan
Editors Fran Bromage, Sarah Parkin, Claire Philip
Designers Jo Cowan, Simon Lee, Andrea Slane
Cover Designer Simon Lee
Production Elizabeth Collins, Caroline Kelly
Reprographics Stephan Davis, Jennifer Barker, Thom Allaway

ISBN 978-1-78209-971-0

Printed in China

British Library Cataloguing-in-Publication Data
A catalogue record for this book is available from the British Library

ACKNOWLEDGEMENTS
The publishers would like to thank the following for the use of their photographs:
Front cover Mike Price/Shutterstock (killer whale), bluehand/Shutterstock (clownfish),
Stephen Rees/Shutterstock (starfish) **Back cover** bluehand/Shutterstock (seahorse)
Dreamstime.com 77 John Anderson; 82 Olga Khoroshunova; 85 Naluphoto
Fotolia.com 54 Vladimir Ovchinnikov; 60 SLDigi; 66 Desertdiver; 71 cbpix
iStockphoto.com 91 Tarasovs **Rex** 68–69 Walt Disney / Everett Collection / Rex Shutterstock
Shutterstock.com 6 ktsdesign; 9 Vilainecrevette; 10 Shutterstock; 11 Mohamed Tazi Cherti; 12 Mogens Trolle;
17 melissaf84; 18 Mariusz Potocki; 19 Heather A. Craig; 20–21(c) Meister Photos; 21(tl) Neil Burton; 22 Spumador;
23 Mariko Yuki; 24 Fotokon; 25 ChameleonsEye; 26 Distinctive Images; 27 Ethan Daniels; 30 JonMilnes;
31(tl) Gustavo Miguel Fernandes, (cr) EpicStockMedia; 36 Roxana Gonzalez; 37 Photodynamic; 40 Shutterstock;
41 javarman; 48 Glenn Price; 50 Jay Hood; 56 Cary Kalscheuer; 58 Niar; 61 Atlaspix; 69 bernd.neeser; 72 NatalieJean;
74 Rich Carey; 78 Levent Konuk; 80 A Cotton Photo; 87 tubuceo; 89 John A. Anderson

All other photographs are from:
digitalSTOCK, digitalvision, Image State, John Foxx, PhotoAlto, PhotoDisc, PhotoEssentials, PhotoPro, Stockbyte

All artworks from the Miles Kelly Artwork Bank

Every effort has been made to acknowledge the source and copyright holder of each picture.
Miles Kelly Publishing apologizes for any unintentional errors or omissions.

Made with paper from a sustainable forest

www.mileskelly.net info@mileskelly.net

Contents

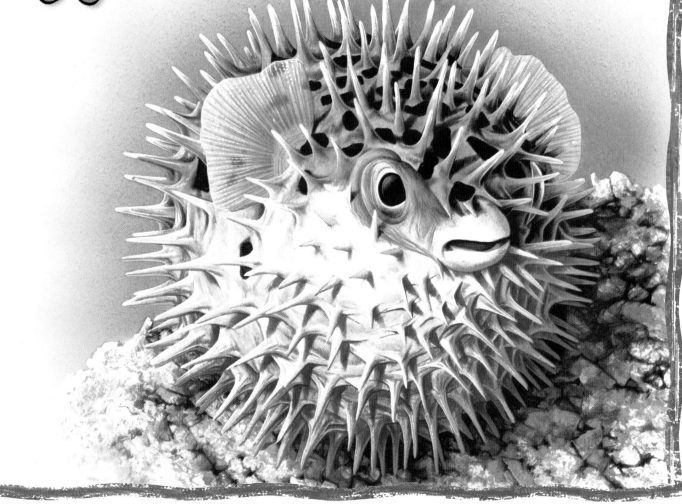

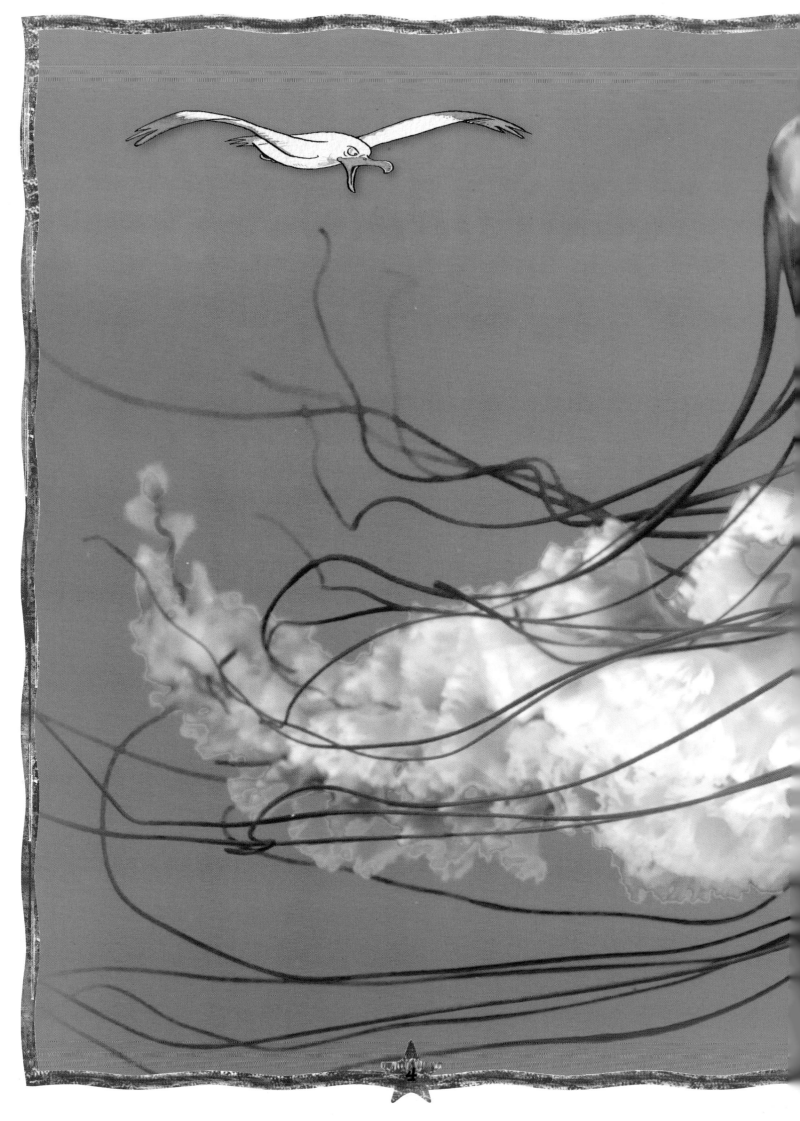

Oceans

Is there only one big ocean?

The Earth is covered by one giant ocean. We split this into five different oceans, which all flow into each other – the Arctic, Atlantic, Pacific, Indian and Southern. The land we live on, the continents, rises out of the oceans. More than two-thirds of the Earth's surface is covered by oceans – there is more than twice as much ocean as land!

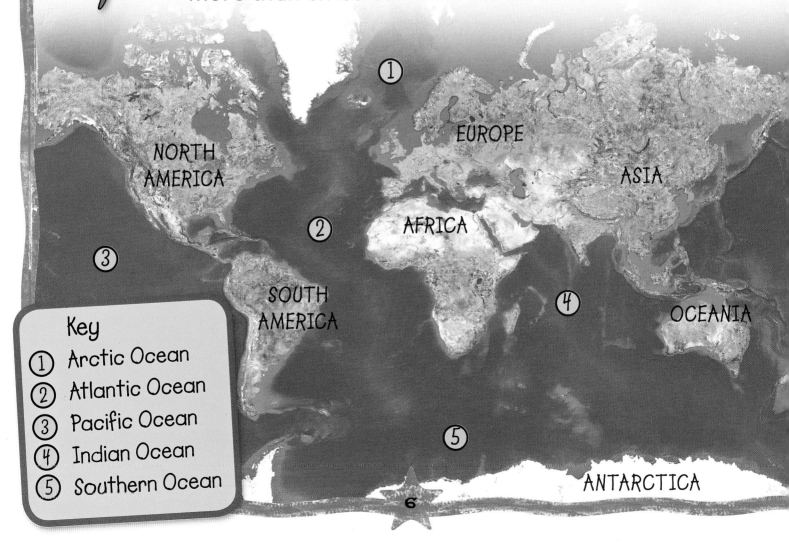

①

EUROPE

NORTH AMERICA

ASIA

②

AFRICA

③

SOUTH AMERICA

④

OCEANIA

⑤

ANTARCTICA

Key

① Arctic Ocean
② Atlantic Ocean
③ Pacific Ocean
④ Indian Ocean
⑤ Southern Ocean

Are there mountains under the sea?

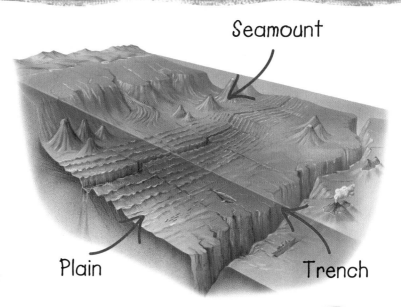

Seamount

Plain

Trench

Yes there are. The land beneath the sea is covered by mountains, flat areas called plains and deep valleys called trenches. There are also huge underwater volcanoes called seamounts.

Salty and fresh

Almost all of the world's water is in the oceans. Only a tiny amount is in freshwater lakes and rivers.

Where do islands come from?

Islands are 'born' beneath the sea. If an underwater volcano erupts, it throws out hot, sticky lava. This cools and hardens in the water. Layers of lava build up and up, until a new island peeps above the waves.

Find

Look at the world map to find where you live. Which ocean is nearest to you?

Island

Do seashells have feet?

Tiny animals called limpets live inside some seashells. They stick to rocks at the shoreline where they eat slimy, green plants called algae. When the tide is out, limpets stick to the rocks like glue, with a strong muscular foot. They only move when the tide crashes in.

Limpets

Can starfish grow arms?

Yes they can. Starfish may have as many as 40 arms, called rays. If a hungry crab grabs hold of one, the starfish abandons its arm, and uses the others to get away. It then begins to grow a new arm.

Anemone

Starfish

Fighting fit

Anemones are a kind of sea-living plant. Some anemones fight over their feeding grounds. Beadlet anemones shoot sharp, tiny hooks at each other until the weakest one gives in.

When is a sponge like an animal?

Sponges are animals! They are simple creatures that filter food from sea water. They can be many different shapes, sizes and colours.

Sponge

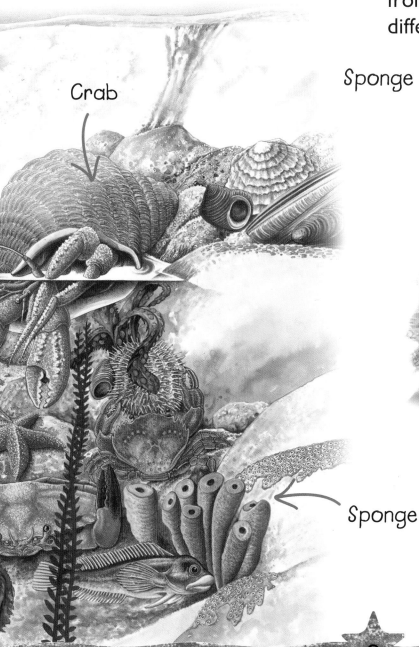

Crab

Sponge

Find

When you next visit a beach, try to find a rockpool. Write a list of what you see.

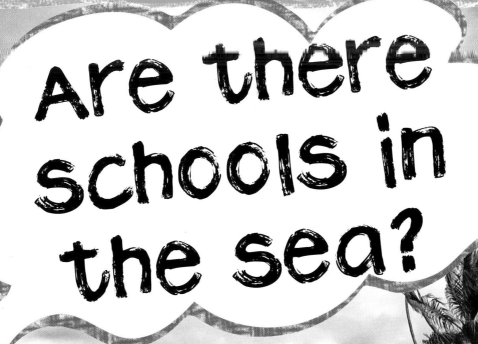

Are there schools in the sea?

Some fish live in big groups called schools. This may protect them from hungry hunters. There are thousands of different types of fish in the sea. Most are covered in shiny scales and use fins and tails to swim. Fish have gills that take in oxygen from the water so that they can breathe.

School of fish

Read

What is a big group of fish called? Read this page to find out.

Which fish looks like an oar?

The oarfish does — and it can grow to be as long as four canoes! It is the longest bony fish and is found in all the world's oceans. Oarfish have a bright red fin along the length of their back. They swim upright through the water.

Oarfish

Flying high

Fish can't survive out of water for long, but flying fish can leap above the waves when swimming at high speed. They look like they are flying as they use their fins to glide through the air.

Sunfish

Do fish like to sunbathe?

Sunfish like sunbathing. Ocean sunfish are huge fish that can weigh up to one tonne — as heavy as a small car! They swim at the surface, as if they're sunbathing.

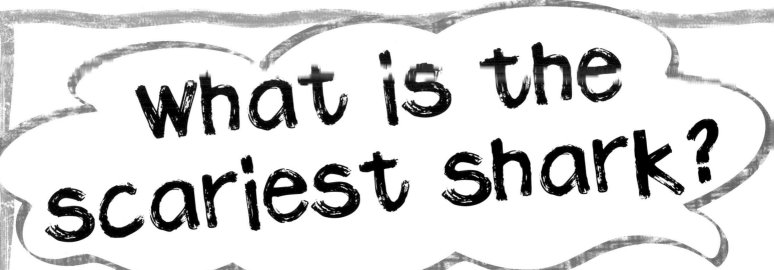

What is the scariest shark?

Great whites are the scariest sharks.
These huge fish speed through the
water at 30 kilometres an hour. Unlike
most fish, the great white shark has
warm blood. This allows its muscles to work well but it
also means that it needs to eat lots of meat. Great
white sharks are fierce hunters. They will
attack and eat almost anything, but
prefer to feed on seals.

Great white shark

when is a whale not a whale?

When it is an orca. Killer whales are also called orcas, but they aren't really whales either – they are the biggest member of the dolphin family. Killer whales will kill and eat almost anything in the ocean from a small fish or seabird, to a large whale.

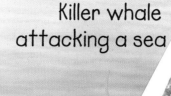

Killer whale attacking a sea

Yum Yum!

Most sharks are meat eaters. Herring are a favourite food for sand tiger and thresher sharks, while a hungry tiger shark will gobble up just about anything!

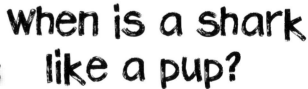

Draw

Using felt-tip pens, draw your own underwater picture. Include a great white shark.

when is a shark like a pup?

When it's a baby. Young sharks are called pups. Some grow inside their mother's body. Others hatch from eggs straight into the sea.

who builds walls beneath the sea?

Tiny animals build underwater walls. These walls are made of coral, the leftover skeletons of tiny sea animals called polyps. Over millions of years, enough skeletons pile up to form walls. These make a coral reef. All kinds of creatures live around a reef.

Seahorse

Parrotfish

LOOK

Do you know where the Great Barrier Reef is? Look carefully in an atlas to find out.

Clownfish

How do fish keep clean?

Cleaner wrasse are little fish that help other fish to keep clean! Larger fish, such as groupers and moray eels, visit the cleaner wrasse, which nibble all the bugs and bits of dirt off the bigger fishes' bodies — what a feast!

Super reef

You can see the Great Barrier Reef from space! At over 2000 kilometres long, it is the largest thing ever built by living creatures.

Lionfish

Coral reef

Cleaner wrasse fish

When is a fish like a clown?

When it's a clownfish. These fish are brightly coloured, like circus clowns. They live among the stinging arms (tentacles) of the sea anemone, where they are safe from enemies.

Sea anemone

Why are whales so big?

Whales have grown to such a huge size because they live in water. The water helps to support their enormous bulk. The blue whale is the biggest animal in the ocean — and the whole planet. It is about 30 metres long and can weigh up to 150 tonnes. Every day, it eats about four tonnes of tiny, shrimp-like creatures called krill.

Blue whale

can whales sing songs?

All whales make sounds, such as squeaks and moans. The male humpback whale seems to sing, probably to attract a mate. He may repeat his song for up to 20 hours!

Humpback whale

stick around!

Barnacles are shellfish. They attach themselves to ships, or the bodies of grey whales and other large sea animals.

measure

The blue whale is 30 metres long. Can you measure how long you are?

Do whales grow tusks?

The narwhal has a tusk like a unicorn's. This tusk is a long, twirly tooth that comes out of the whale's head. The males use their tusks as weapons when they fight over females. The tusk can grow to 3 metres in length.

Do lions live in the sea?

There are lions in the sea, but not the furry, roaring kind. Sea lions, seals and walruses are all warm-blooded animals that have adapted to ocean life. They have flippers instead of legs – far more useful for swimming. A thick layer of fat under the skin keeps them warm in cold water.

Think

What do you think whales, dolphins and seals have in common with humans?

Seals

18

who sleeps in seaweed?

Sea otters do! They live in forests of giant seaweed, called kelp. When they sleep, they wrap strands of kelp around their bodies to stop themselves being washed out to sea.

Sea otter

Singing seal!

Leopard seals sing in their sleep! These seals, found in the Antarctic, chirp and whistle while they snooze.

can a walrus change colour?

Walruses seem to change colour. In cold water, a walrus can look pale brown or even white. This is because blood drains from the skin to stop the body losing heat. On land, blood returns to the skin and the walrus looks pink!

Are there crocodiles in the sea?

Most crocodiles live in rivers and swamps. The saltwater crocodile also swims out to sea — it doesn't seem to mind the salty water. These crocodiles are huge, and can grow to be 7 metres long and one tonne in weight.

Saltwater crocodile

Find

Turtles only come ashore for one reason. Can you do some research and find out why?

which lizard loves to swim?

Most lizards live on land, where it is easier to warm up their cold-blooded bodies. Marine iguanas depend on the sea for food and dive underwater to eat seaweed. When they are not diving, they sit on rocks to soak up the sunshine.

Marine iguana

How deep can a turtle dive?

Leatherback turtles can dive up to 1200 metres for their dinner. They are the biggest sea turtles and they make the deepest dives. Leatherbacks feed mostly on jellyfish but also eat crabs, lobsters and starfish.

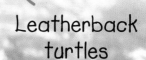

Leatherback turtles

slithery snakes

There are poisonous snakes in the sea. The banded sea snake and the yellow-bellied sea snake both use poison to kill their prey. Their poison is far stronger than that of land snakes.

Do seabirds dig burrows?

Most seabirds make nests on cliffs.
The puffin digs a burrow on the clifftop,
like a rabbit. Sometimes, a puffin even
takes over an empty rabbit hole.
Here it lays its egg. Both parents look
after the chick when it hatches.

Think
Sea birds have
webbed feet. Why
do you think this
is? Do you have
webbed feet?

Puffins

Wandering albatross

Can seabirds sleep as they fly?

Wandering albatrosses are the biggest seabirds and spend months at sea. They are very good gliders, and even sleep as they fly. To feed, they sit on the surface of the water and catch creatures such as squid. An albatross has a wingspan of around 3 metres – about the length of a family car!

HOP on over

The smallest seabird is the Wilson's storm petrel, at just 16 to 19 centimetres long. It is found over the Atlantic, Indian and Antarctic Oceans. This petrel hops over the water's surface, snatching tiny sea creatures to eat.

Blue-footed booby

which birds like to dance?

Boobies are seabirds that live in large groups. The males have bright red or blue feet. When they are looking for a mate, they dance in front of the female, to attract her with their colourful feet!

How do polar bears learn to swim?

Polar bears are good swimmers and they live around the freezing Arctic Ocean. They learn to swim when they are cubs, by following their mother into the water. With their big front paws, the bears paddle through the water. They can swim for many hours.

Polar bear

Imagine
Pretend to be a polar bear. Imagine what life is like at the North Pole.

Are penguins fast swimmers?

Penguins are birds – but they cannot fly. All penguins are fast swimmers. The fastest swimmer is the gentoo penguin. It can reach speeds of 27 kilometres an hour underwater.

Gentoo penguin

Small and tall!

The smallest penguin is the fairy penguin at just 40 centimetres tall. The biggest is the emperor penguin at 1.3 metres in height – as tall as a seven-year-old child!

Emperor penguins

which penguin dad likes to babysit?

Emperor penguin dads look after the chicks. The female lays an egg and leaves her mate to keep it warm. The male balances the egg on his feet to keep it off the ice. He goes without food until the chick hatches. When it does, the mother returns and both parents care for it.

Is seaweed good to eat?

Seaweed can be very good to eat. In shallow, warm seawater, people can grow their own seaweed. It is then dried in the sun, which helps to keep it fresh. Seaweed is even used to make ice cream!

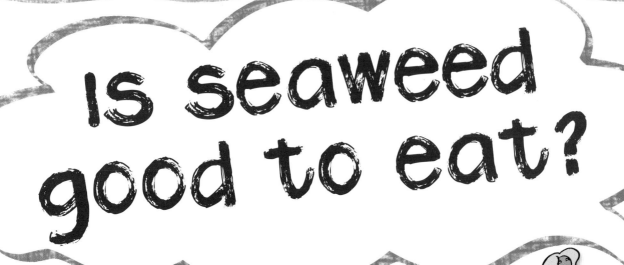

Collecting seaweed

List

Make a list of the things you can eat from the ocean. Which foods have you tried before?

How do we get salt from the sea?

Sea water is salty. Salt is an important substance. In hot, low-lying areas, people build walls to hold shallow pools of sea water. The water dries up in the sun, leaving behind crystals of salt.

How are lobsters caught?

Lobsters are large, edible shellfish. Fishermen catch them in wooden cages called pots. Attracted to dead fish put in the pots, lobsters push the door of the pot open to reach the fish. But once inside, the lobster can't get out again.

Lobster pot

Pearly oysters

Pearls grow inside oysters. If a grain of sand gets stuck in an oyster's shell, it irritates it. The oyster slowly coats the grain with a substance that is used to line the inside of its shell. As more coats are added, a pearl forms.

Are there chimneys under the sea?

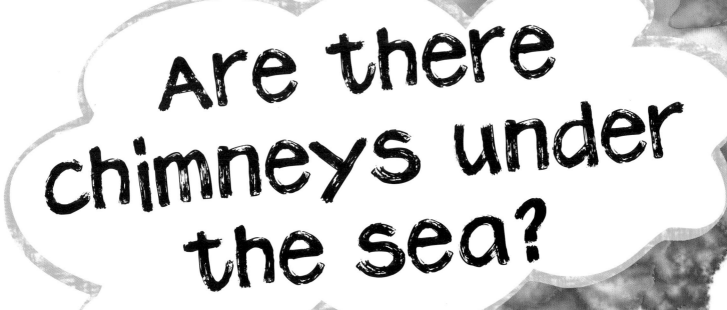

Rocky chimneys on the ocean floor give off clouds of hot water. These chimneys lie deep beneath the ocean. The hot water feeds strange creatures, such as tube worms and sea spiders.

Rat tail fish

watery village

In 1963, diver Jacques Cousteau built a village on the bed of the Red Sea. Along with four other divers, he lived there for a whole month.

Giant clams

Do monsters live in the sea?

Sea monsters do not exist. Long ago, people thought they did. The giant squid may have been mistaken for a monster. It has long arms called tentacles, and eyes as big as dinner plates.

Squid

what is a mermaid?

Mermaids are strange creatures with the body of a woman and a long fishy tail — but they aren't real. People once thought they lived in the sea and confused sailors with their beautiful singing.

Chimney

Sea spider

Tube worms

write

Can you think of any stories or films about mermaids? Why don't you try and write your own?

How do divers breathe underwater?

Divers have a spare pair of lungs.
Scuba divers carry a special piece of
breathing equipment called an 'aqua
lung'. These are tanks filled with oxygen
(air) that sit on the divers' backs. A
long tube supplies the diver with air.

Aqua lung

Diver

wear
Try wearing some
goggles in the bath.
Pop in some toys
and see what they
look like under
the water.

what is a jetski?

A jetski is like a motorbike without wheels that travels on water. It pushes out a jet of water behind it, which pushes it forward. Some jetskiers can reach speeds of 100 kilometres an hour.

Jetski

Can people ride the waves?

Yes they can, on surfboards. Surfing became popular in the 1950s. Modern surfboards are made of super-light material. People stand up on their surfboards and ride the waves. The best places to surf are off the coasts of Mexico and Hawaii.

Surfer

water record!

A single boat towed 100 waterskiers! This record was made off the coast of Australia in 1986 and no one has beaten it yet. The drag boat was a cruiser called 'Reef Cat'.

Quiz time

page 11

Do you remember what you have read about oceans? Here are some questions to test your memory. The pictures will help you. If you get stuck, read the pages again.

3. Which fish looks like an oar?

4. When is a whale not a whale?

page 13

1. Are there mountains under the sea?

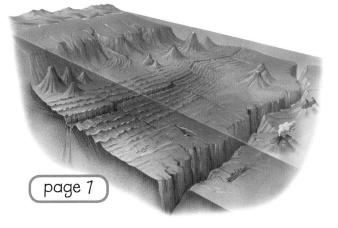

page 7

page 17

5. Do whales grow tasks?

2. When is a sponge like an animal?

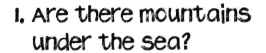

page 9

page 19

6. Who sleeps in seaweed?

7. Are there crocodiles in the sea?

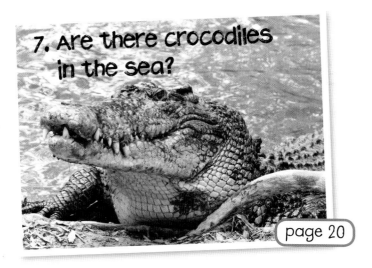

page 20

page 26

11. Is seaweed good to eat?

8. Can seabirds sleep as they fly?

page 23

12. What is a mermaid?

page 29

9. How do polar bears learn to swim?

page 24

page 30

13. How do divers breathe underwater?

page 25

10. Which penguin dad likes to babysit?

Answers

1. Yes, there are
2. A sponge is an animal
3. The oarfish
4. When it's a killer whale, which is actually a member of the dolphin family
5. Yes, the narwhal has a tusk
6. The sea otter
7. The saltwater crocodile swims in the sea
8. Yes, the wandering albatross can
9. By following their mother into the water
10. The emperor penguin
11. Yes, it can be
12. A creature that is half-woman, half-fish
13. By using an aqua lung

Seashore

How long is the seashore?

Around the world there are thousands of kilometres of seashore. It can be sandy, pebbly, muddy, or rocky with high cliffs. Many interesting plants and animals make their homes on or near the shore – and so do millions of people.

Sandy seashore

Which shores are the coldest?

The coldest seashores are around the North and South poles, the chilliest ends of the Earth. It is so cold here that the sea often freezes. Polar bears, penguins and seals are good at surviving on these icy shores.

Crabeater seal

Find out
Do you live by the sea? If not, look on a map to find your nearest seashore.

Trees in the breeze

Seashores can be blasted by winds from the sea that constantly blow in the same direction. These winds can make trees grow over to one side.

Why do seashores have tides?

Because the Earth is spinning! As Earth spins, the Moon pulls on the sea, and the surface rises. Water flows up the shore, making a high tide. Then it flows out again, creating a low tide. Each seashore has two high tides a day.

Why do seashells cling to rocks?

They cling to rocks so they don't get washed away by the tide. Animals such as limpets, mussels and barnacles live inside seashells. At high tide they open their shells to find food. At low tide, the shells shut tight so they don't dry out.

Limpet

Barnacles

Mussels

What are seashore zones?

The area between high and low tide is called the intertidal zone. Low tide zone is wettest, and has lots of seaweed. High tide zone is drier, and has more land plants.

Fun at the beach

Sandy beaches make a great place for sports, such as horseriding, kite-flying, football and volleyball.

How big are the biggest waves?

Winds make waves, which break onto the seashore. Some waves can be 30 metres high – taller than a tower of 18 people. The biggest waves are tsunamis, caused by earthquakes shaking the sea. The tallest ever was 500 metres high!

what is a coral reef?

A coral reef is a stony structure found in shallow oceans. Tiny animals called polyps build up layers of hard, colourful coral over many years, to use as a home. A reef also makes a good home for other sea creatures, such as fish, rays, octopuses, turtles and crabs.

Coral reef

Why do crabs walk sideways?

If crabs want to move quickly, walking sideways is best! Their flat, wide bodies help them slip into narrow hiding places. This means that their legs only bend sideways. Crabs can walk forwards, but only very slowly.

Sharks in the shallows

Some sharks, like the black-tip reef shark, are often found swimming around coral reefs in search of a snack.

Do all crabs have shells?

Most crabs have a hard shell, but hermit crabs don't. They need to find some kind of 'shell' to protect their soft bodies. Usually, they use another sea creature's old empty shell.

Christmas Island red crab

Make

Using modelling clay, make a hermit crab and give it a home from a shell, cup or plastic lid.

Why do birds love the seaside?

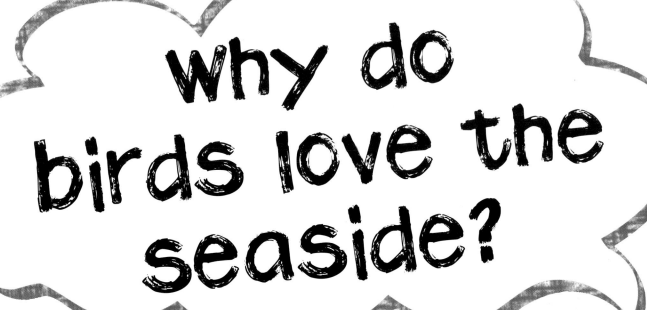

Great black-backed gull

Lesser black-backed gull

Herring gull

Rock dove

Chough

Guillemot

Razorbill

Puffin

Many kinds of seabird live on and near the seashore. It's a good place to find food and raise their chicks. Seabirds make their nests on the shore or on rocky cliff ledges. They fly out over the water to catch fish.

Do beetles head for the beach?

The tiger beetle does! This shiny, green beetle lays its eggs in warm, sandy places. These beetles are often found in sand dunes – small, grassy hills of sand at the top of a beach.

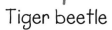
Tiger beetle

Paint
Copy the picture on this page and paint a tiger beetle. Add green glitter for its shiny body.

Swimming cats
Some tigers live in mangrove forests near the coast. They like to splash in the water to cool down.

How does being sick help a chick?

Fulmars are seabirds. When they go fishing, they leave their chicks alone in their nests. If hunting animals come near the nests, the chicks squirt stinky, fishy, oily vomit to scare them away!

can you tell a pebble from an egg?

You might not be able to! The ringed plover lays its speckled eggs on pebbly beaches, where they blend in so well they're almost impossible to see. This helps to keep the eggs safe from animals that might eat them.

Eggs

Think

Apart from birds, can you think of any other animals that lay eggs? Use a book to help you.

Which bird hangs its wings out to dry?

The cormorant dives to catch fish. Its feathers soak up the water, making it easier to stay underwater to hunt. After fishing, the cormorant spreads its wings to dry them out.

Cormorant

Elephants of the seashore

'Sea elephants' are actually a type of seal. They are called elephant seals because they have a big droopy nose a bit like a trunk.

How fast can a gannet dive?

Gannets fish by flying above the sea, then plunging down. They fold their wings behind them, making a rocket shape, and can hit the water at 100 kilometres an hour! This lets them dive deep into the water.

Does the seashore have shapes?

Sea stacks

Arch

Yes, seashores have lots of shapes. There are bays, spits, cliffs, archways and towers. They form over many years, as wind and waves batter the coast. Softer rocks get carved away into bays and hollows. Harder rocks last longer, and form sticking-out headlands.

Shingle spit

Shingle beach

Make

At a pebbly beach, make a sculpture by balancing small pebbles on top of each other in a tower.

Bay

why are pebbles round?

The pebbles on beaches are stones that have been rolled and tumbled around by waves. As they knock together, they lose their sharp corners and edges, and slowly become smooth and round.

Cave

Cliffs

what is sand made of?

Sand is made of tiny pieces of rocks and shells. Larger lumps gradually break down into grains, as the waves crash onto them and make them swirl around.

Delta

Sandy beach

plastic sand

On some beaches, one in every ten sand grains is actually made of plastic. It comes from litter dropped on beaches or thrown from boats.

Why is a curlew's beak so long?

To find its food buried in the mud, a curlew needs a long, thin beak! It sticks its beak deep into the mud to pick out worms, crabs and insects. A curlew also has long legs to wade in the water.

Curlew

Measure

With a long ruler, mark out one square metre. Try to imagine thousands of seashells living in this area!

Are seashells different shapes?

Yes, they are. A seashell's shape depends on the creature that lives in it, and how it feeds and moves. Spireshells and tower shells are spirals. Clams and cockles have two hinged shells. They open them to feed, or close them to keep safe.

Clam

Tower shell

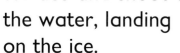
Laver spireshell

Common cockle

Painted top shell

How do penguins get out of the water?

Penguins can't fly, but they can swim fast underwater, using their wings as flippers. When they want to get out of the sea, they zoom up to the surface and shoot out of the water, landing on the ice.

crowds of creatures

Some muddy beaches have more then 50,000 tiny shellfish living in each square metre of mud.

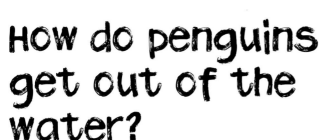

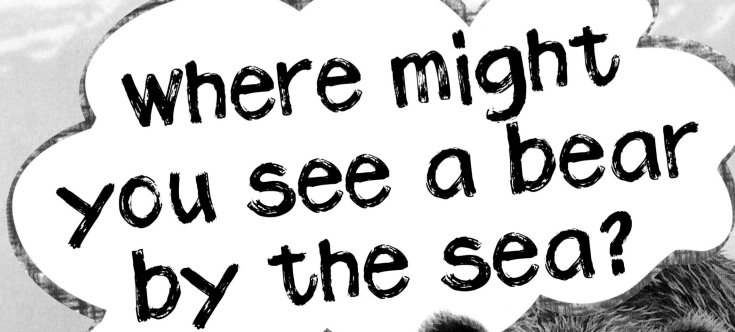

where might you see a bear by the sea?

You might see a bear at an estuary, the place where a river meets the sea. In parts of Canada and the United States, grizzly bears try to catch salmon as they leave the sea and head up rivers to breed. They may also nibble berries and sea plants.

Grizzly bear

what is sea pink?

Sea pink is a seashore flower. Not many plants can survive near the sea because it's so windy and salty. But sea pink is tough. It also has special parts that carry salt out of the plant through its leaves.

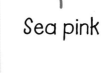

Sea pink

Down in one

Penguins swallow fish whole, and the fish dissolve inside their stomachs. They can bring the mush back up to feed their chicks.

Why does glass come from the seashore?

Make

Try some baby penguin food! Mash tinned tuna with a teaspoon of olive oil, and eat it in a sandwich!

Because it's made from sand! Glass is made by heating sand until it melts and turns clear. Long ago, people burnt sea plants such as glasswort to get chemicals for glass-making.

51

What hides in the sand?

Worms, shrimps, razorshells and some crabs all burrow down into the sand to hide. At high tide they come out and feed. At low tide, being under the sand helps them to stay damp, and avoid being eaten.

Gull

Shrimps

HUNT

Go on a beach treasure hunt. Look for different shells, different-coloured pebbles and seaweed.

Razorshell

Worms

where is the highest tide in the world?

At the Bay of Fundy in Canada, high tide is super-high! The sea level rises to around 17 metres higher than at low tide. At most beaches, the water is just 2 to 3 metres deeper at high tide.

Treasure-hunting

People love beachcombing too. It's fun to look for interesting creatures, pebbles, shells, or bits of glass that have been rubbed smooth by the sea.

Otter

Lizard

Toad

Crab

which animals go beachcombing?

A line of seaweed, driftwood, shells and litter usually collects at the 'strandline' – the level the high tide flows up to. Seabirds, and other animals such as foxes and otters, go 'beachcombing' along the strandline to look for washed-up crabs and fish to eat.

what is a lagoon?

A lagoon is a bit like a shallow lake, but filled with salty seawater. They form when part of the sea is surrounded by a sandbar or a coral reef. Lagoons are warm, shallow and protected from storms – so they make great homes for wildlife.

Lagoon

Make
Build your own sandcastle at the beach or in a sandpit. How tall can you make it?

Which fish can walk on land?

Mudskippers are fish, but they can walk on land! They live in the intertidal zone and can breathe in air or water. They skip over the sand or mud, using their front fins like feet.

Mudskipper

Stingers!

Anemones are seashore creatures with stinging tentacles. They grab and sting prey, then gobble it up!

Why do flamingos have long legs?

Flamingos are very tall, pink wading birds. Their long, thin legs help them walk through shallow water in lagoons. They dip their beaks into the water, and use them like a sieve to catch shrimps.

when can you see a rock pool?

When the tide goes out you might see a rock pool. Seawater gets trapped in hollows in rocks or sand. The best places to find rock pools are rocky beaches. Sea creatures shelter here at low tide.

Rock pool

Are there fleas at the beach?

No, there aren't any fleas, but there are little creatures that look like them. Sand hoppers stay buried in the sand all day, then come out at night to look for food.

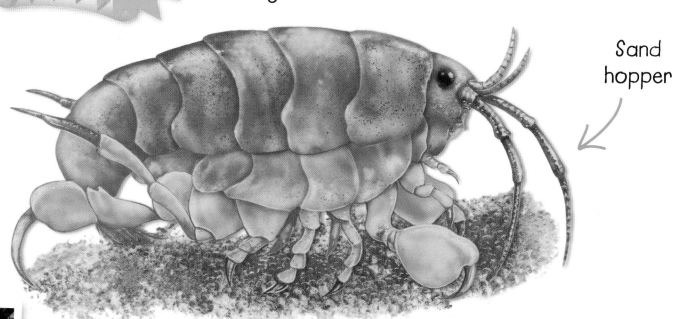

Sand hopper

What lives in a rock pool?

All kinds of creatures live in a rock pool. These can include crabs, sea anemones, sea urchins, shrimps, shellfish, starfish, sponges, small fish and even octopuses. There are also seaweeds, which animals can hide under.

Super sponges
Rock pool sponges are actually simple animals! The natural sponge that you might use in the bath is a long-dead, dried-out sponge!

which forest grows in the sea?

Mangroves are trees that grow in salty water or seaside mud. Some seashores, especially in hot, tropical places, have mangrove forests growing along them. The mangroves' roots stick out of the ground, and get covered by the tide when it comes in.

Mangroves

Why do crabs turn the ground bright red?

When red crabs march, they turn the ground into a red, moving mass! These crabs live on Christmas Island in the Indian Ocean. Twice a year, thousands of red crabs head to the sea to lay eggs. Then they go back to their forest homes.

Red crabs

PLAY
Have a crab race with your friends. You're only allowed to run sideways, like a crab!

Fishy cat

In South East Asia there is a wild cat that goes fishing. The fishing cat is a good swimmer, and hunts for fish and other small animals in mangrove swamps.

What is a sea cow?

Sea cows aren't really cows. They are dugongs and manatees – huge, sausage-shaped sea creatures, a bit like seals. Like a real cow, sea cows graze on plants, such as sea grass and mangrove leaves.

59

where do turtles lay their eggs?

Sea turtles live in the sea, but lay their eggs on land. Female turtles crawl up sandy beaches at night, and dig holes with their flippers, in which they lay their eggs. Then they cover them over with sand, and leave them to hatch.

Turtle

Salty nose

The marine iguana is a lizard that swims in the sea. As it rests on rocks to warm up, salt from the sea makes a white patch on its nose.

Why do baby turtles race to the sea?

When turtle eggs hatch, baby turtles climb out of their sandy nest and head for the sea. They must reach the water quickly, before they get gobbled up by a seabird, crab or fox.

Find out

There are different types of turtle. Look in books or on the Internet to find out what they are.

Which seabird has a colourful beak?

Puffins have bright beaks striped with orange, yellow and black. In spring, their beaks and feet become brighter, to help them find a mate. Males and females rub their beaks together to show they like each other.

Puffins

Quiz time

Do you remember what you have read about the seashore? Here are some questions to test your memory. The pictures will help you. If you get stuck, read the pages again.

1. How long is the seashore?

page 36

2. How big are the biggest waves?

page 39

3. Do beetles head for the beach?

page 43

4. Can you tell a pebble from an egg?

page 44

5. Why are pebbles round?

page 47

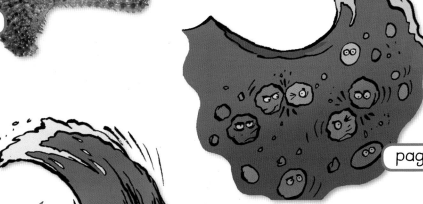

6. Are seashells different shapes?

page 49

page 49

7. How do penguins get out of the water?

page 51

11. Are there fleas at the beach? page 57

12. What is a sea cow? page 59

8. Why does glass come from the seashore?

13. Why do baby turtles race to the sea?

page 61

9. What hides in the sand?

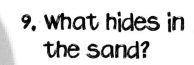

page 52

Answers

1. Thousands of kilometres long
2. The biggest waves (tsunamis) can be 30 metres high
3. The tiger beetle does
4. You might not be able to, the ringed plover lays eggs that look like pebbles
5. Because they have been rolled and tumbled around by waves
6. Yes they are
7. They zoom up to the surface and shoot out of the water
8. Because it's made from sand
9. Worms, shrimps, razorshells and some crabs
10. The mudskipper
11. No, but there are sandhoppers
12. Dugongs and manatees
13. To avoid being gobbled up by predators

10. Which fish can walk on land?

page 55

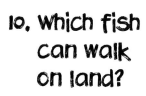

Coral Reef

Is a coral reef alive?

Coral reefs are living structures that grow in the sea. They are built by millions of tiny animals, called coral polyps. When they die, new polyps grow on top. This builds up layers of coral rock over time. Some reefs, such as the Great Barrier Reef, are enormous and can be seen from the air.

Great Barrier Reef

Coral

Do trees grow underwater?

Trees do not grow underwater, but soft tree corals look like trees because they have branches. Coral reefs are sometimes called 'rainforests of the sea'. Like rainforests on land, coral reefs are important homes for millions of marine animals.

Soft tree coral

Big brains

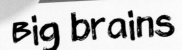

Octopuses are super smart animals that live near reefs. They are experts at finding prey hiding in rocky crevices.

Draw

Choose your favourite fish from this book. Draw it onto paper and colour it in.

How do coral polyps feed?

Coral polyps live in hard, stony cups and feed on tiny animals that drift by in the water. They catch food with tiny stingers on their tentacles, as do jellyfish, which are in the same animal family as coral polyps.

can turtles swim far?

Turtles go on very long journeys across the sea to feed, mate or lay their eggs. Female turtles always return to the same beach to lay their eggs. How they find their way is still a mystery, but they don't seem to get lost!

Discover

Use an atlas to find out which country beginning with 'A' is near the Great Barrier Reef.

Turtles from *Finding Nemo*

When does a fish look like a stone?

When it is a stonefish! These fish are almost impossible to see when they are lying flat and still on the seabed. Their colours blend in with the rocky and sandy surfaces.

Stonefish

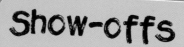

Show-offs

Cuttlefish can change colour! In just a few seconds, a cuttlefish can flash colours of red, yellow, brown or black.

Do seahorses gallop?

Seahorses are fish, not horses, so they cannot run or gallop. They are not very good swimmers so they wrap their tails around seaweed to stop ocean currents carrying them away.

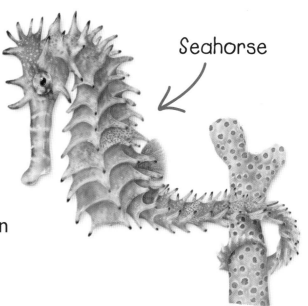

Seahorse

69

Why are fish like lions?

Lionfish

Some fish are like lions because they hunt for food at night. Lionfish hide among rocks in the day. As the sun sets, they come out to hunt for small animals to eat. They have amazing stripes and spines on their bodies. Their spines hold venom, which can cause very painful stings.

Dive and stay alive
Divers can use cages to watch sharks safely. The divers wear masks and carry tanks that have air inside them so they can breathe underwater.

when do birds visit reefs?

Birds visit coral reef islands to build their nests. When their eggs hatch, the birds find plenty of fish at the reef to feed to their chicks. Albatrosses are large sea birds, so their chicks need lots of fish!

count

If an albatross chick needs to eat two big fish every day, how many fish will it eat in five days?

can slugs be pretty?

Yes they can! Like many coral reef animals, sea slugs have amazing colours and patterns. These warn other animals that they are harmful to eat. Most sea slugs are small, but some can grow to 30 centimetres in length.

Sea slugs

What lives on a reef?

A huge number of different animals live on or around reefs. They are home to fish of all shapes and sizes, including sharks. There are many other animals too — octopus, squid, slugs, sponges, starfish and urchins all live on reefs.

Sea grasses

Black sea urchin

Sea turtle

Starfish

Which sea creature eats weeds?

Sea urchins help to keep the reef healthy by grazing on algae, seagrasses and seaweed. If there is too much seaweed on a reef, it can block the light, which the coral polyps need to grow.

A sting in the tail

Blue-spotted rays live in coral reefs and feed on shellfish, crabs and worms. They have stinging spines on their tails.

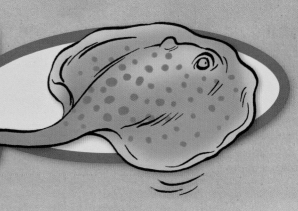

Measure

Every year coral reefs grow about 10 centimetres. How much have you grown in a year?

What do coral reefs need to grow?

The polyps that build up coral reefs need plenty of sunlight and clean water to grow. They mostly live in shallow water near land where sunlight can reach them.

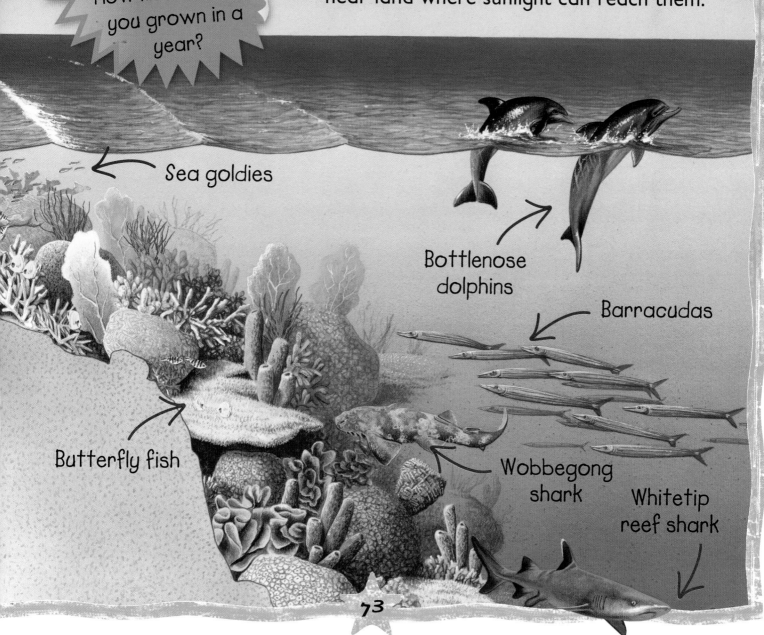

Sea goldies

Bottlenose dolphins

Barracudas

Butterfly fish

Wobbegong shark

Whitetip reef shark

can parrots swim?

Of course not – parrots are birds that live in jungles! Parrotfish, however, are dazzling, colourful fish that swim around reefs, nibbling at the coral. They have beak-like mouths, which is why they are named after parrots.

Parrotfish

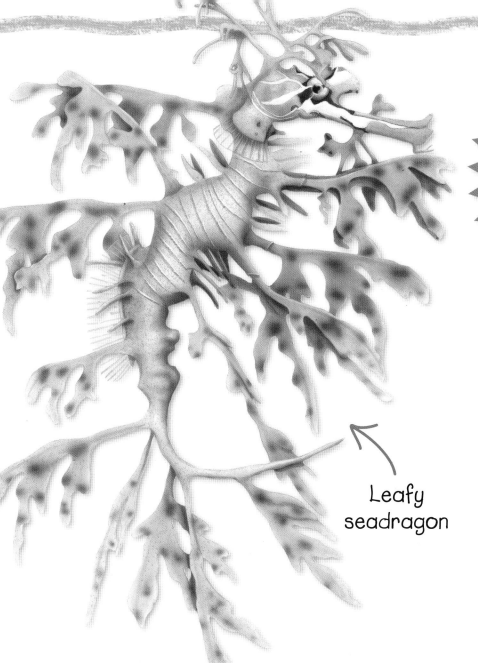

Leafy
seadragon

Think

Make up a story about a leafy seadragon and a parrotfish. Draw pictures to tell your story.

Which animal looks like seaweed?

A type of seahorse called a leafy seadragon does. Its strange shape makes it hard to spot when it swims around seaweed, hiding it from big fish that might want to eat it.

Do sponges help build reefs?

Sometimes – sponges are animals that bore, or dig, holes into coral. This can weaken a reef. However, when sponges die their bodies build up extra layers, which add to the reef structure.

Deadly jelly

Box jellyfish have deadly stings on their tentacles. Divers and swimmers stay away from them.

Why does an octopus have eight arms?

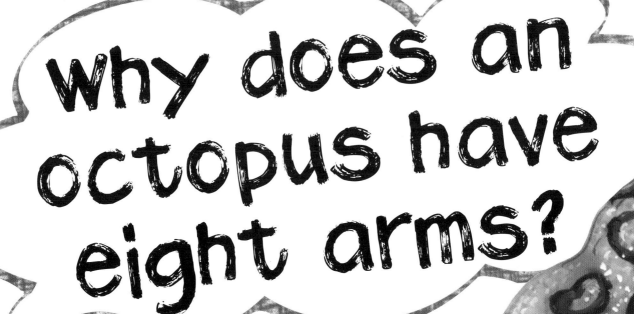

Having eight arms allows an octopus to move quickly and grab food to eat. Each arm has suction cups that can grip onto things. An octopus grabs food with its eight strong arms, and pulls it towards its mouth.

Make
Draw lots of pictures of coral reef animals and stick them on a large piece of card to make a poster.

Blue-ringed octopus

Who looks after a seahorse's eggs?

Females lay the eggs, but the males look after them in a special pouch on the front of their bodies. This keeps the eggs safe from bigger fish that might eat them. When the eggs hatch, the babies swim out of the pouch.

Don't eat me!

Little coral polyps live next to each other, but they do not always get on. Sometimes one polyp might eat its neighbour!

Do christmas trees grow on reefs?

Christmas trees do not grow on reefs – but Christmas tree worms do. These little animals live in burrows inside the reef. The feathery, spiral parts we can see are called feeding tentacles.

Christmas tree worm

where do clownfish live?

Clownfish live in the tentacles of coral reef creatures called sea anemones. Like coral polyps, these strange-looking animals sting their prey. Clownfish have a slimy skin covering that protects them from the sting and allows them to live there unharmed.

Sea anemone

Hide

Invite some friends to join you in a game of hide and seek. Where could you hide?

Clownfish

shark attack

Some coral sharks aren't aggressive and people can feed them by hand. Bull sharks aren't so relaxed and have been know to attack divers.

can seashells be deadly?

The coneshell can be. The shell is just the animal's hard outer casing — it is the soft-bodied creature inside that is the dangerous part. Coneshells hunt other animals and attack by jabbing them with a deadly venom.

Coneshell

which shrimp likes to punch its prey?

Mantis shrimps may be small, but they can pack a big punch. They live in reefs near Australia and in the Pacific Ocean. They punch their prey to stun it, and then tuck in to a tasty meal.

can starfish be blue?

Most starfish are red or brown, but big blue ones live on some reefs. Starfish have small, tube-like feet on the undersides of their arms, which allow them to crawl over the reef. They have tiny eyes at the end of each arm, which can only see light or dark.

Starfish

Make

Make a map that shows where pirate treasure is buried on a coral island.

Do jellyfish wobble?

No, jellyfish may look like jelly, but they are living animals. They have long, stinging tentacles that hang below their bodies as they swim. Some jellyfish live around coral reefs, where there are plenty of fish to eat.

Box jellyfish

Fish hotspot

There are more than 24,000 different types of fish in the world. Many of those live in or around coral reefs.

Why did pirates bury treasure on coral islands?

Pirates are believed to have buried stolen treasure so no one could find it. There are lots of stories about pirates who buried gold and precious stones on coral islands, but we don't know how true these tales are.

why are corals different shapes?

The shape a coral grows into depends on the type of polyp it has. Where the coral grows on the reef is also important. Brain coral grows slowly and in calm water. Staghorn and elkhorn corals grow more quickly, and in shallow water.

Brain coral

Elkhorn coral

Staghorn coral

Are there butterflies in the sea?

There is a type of butterfly living in the sea – but it isn't an insect, it's a fish! Many butterfly fish have colourful spots and stripes to help make them hard to spot.

Butterfly fish

LOOK
Find out if you can see colours better in the dark or in the light.

Going for a spin
Dolphins visit coral reefs to feast on fish. They jump out of the water and can even spin, though no one knows why they do it.

can fish see in the dark?

Many animals can see in the dark. Lots of coral animals sleep during the day, but at night they come out to look for food or mates. Many, such as the red soldierfish, are much better at seeing in the dark than people are.

which crab moves house?

Hermit crabs live inside borrowed shells and move house if they find a bigger, better one. They don't have their own shells so they have to find one to protect their soft bodies. Most hermit crabs choose snail shells to live in.

Hermit
crab →

why is some coral white?

Most coral is very colourful, until it dies and turns white or grey. There are many reasons why corals are dying. Dirty water is one of the most important reasons. Water that is too warm is also bad for polyps.

Damaged coral

Slow-growers

Giant clams can grow to be enormous – up to 150 centimetres long! They can live for 70 years.

Measure

Use a measuring tape to find out how long a giant clam is.

who looks after coral reefs?

Special ocean parks are set up to look after the animals that live on coral reefs. People are not allowed to catch the fish or damage the reef inside these protected areas.

Why do coral fish dance?

To attract the attention of fish who might need a clean! Bluestreak cleaner wrasses feed on the parasites that attach themselves to the bodies of fish. When the wrasses are hungry, they dance around bigger fish, like moray eels, to let them know they are ready to clean.

Moray eel

Whale shark

Are all sharks dangerous?

No, most sharks would never attack a person. Whale sharks are huge but they don't eat big animals. They swim through the water with their large mouths open. They suck in water and any little creatures swimming in it.

Which crab wears boxing gloves?

Boxer crabs hold sea anemones in their claws, like boxing gloves. They wave them at any animals that come too close – the sight of the stinging tentacles warns other animals to stay away.

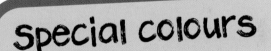
Wrasse

Brush

We don't have wrasses, so when you brush your teeth try hard to remove every tiny bit of food.

Special colours

Coral fish come in amazing colours and patterns. Good looks are important for survival. Blue and yellow fish look bright to us, but they are hidden on the reef by the way the sunlight is reflected.

Do sharks use hammers?

No, but some sharks have heads that look like hammers! These strange-looking sharks have wide, flattened heads. The shape might help them to find food, swim fast or change direction easily.

Hammerhead shark

Do squid change colour?

Yes, squid and octopuses are able to change colour, so they can hide, or send messages to each other. They can change colour very quickly – in just one or two seconds.

Caribbean reef squid

world wonder

No one had studied the Great Barrier Reef or the wildlife that lived on it until British explorer James Cook (1728–1779) sailed his ship right onto the reef, in 1770.

which fish are shocking?

Electric rays can shock other animals by making electric charges in their bodies. As they swim over other fish, they stun them with powerful jolts of electricity. The rays then eat their prey whole, headfirst!

Dress

We change the way we look with the clothes we wear. How quickly can you change clothes?

which fish is spiky?

Pufferfish are strange-looking, poisonous fish with sharp spines. When they feel scared, pufferfish blow up their bodies to make their spines stand on end. This makes them bigger and much harder to swallow.

Pufferfish with spines relaxed

Pufferfish with spines on end

March

Imagine you are a lobster on a long march. How far can you march before you get tired?

Why do lobsters march?

Coral reef spiny lobsters march to deep, dark water where they lay their eggs. They march through the night at the end of the summer. Thousands of lobsters join the march to reach a safe place to breed.

clean teeth.

When fish such as sweetlips want their teeth cleaned, they swim to find wrasse fish and open their mouths.

Crown-of-thorns starfish

HOW do starfish eat their prey?

Starfish turn their mouths inside out to eat. The crown-of-thorns starfish kills coral by eating the soft polyps inside. Each of these large starfish can have up to 21 arms.

Quiz time

Do you remember what you have read about coral reefs? Here are some questions to test your memory. The pictures will help you. If you get stuck, read the pages again.

3. Why are fish like lions?

page 70

4. Which sea creature eats weeds?

page 72

1. Do trees grow underwater?

5. Which animal looks like seaweed?

page 75

page 67

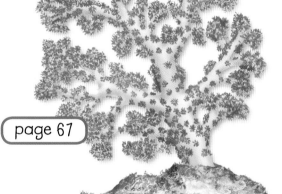

page 69

2. When does a fish look like a stone?

6. Who looks after a seahorse's eggs?

page 77

7. Where do clownfish live?

page 78

8. Do jellyfish wobble?

page 81

9. Can fish see in the dark?

page 83

10. Who looks after coral reefs?

11. Which crab wears boxing gloves?

page 87

12. Which fish are shocking?

page 89

13. Why do lobsters march?

page 91

Answers

1. No, but some corals have branches like trees
2. When it is a stonefish
3. Because they are hunters and come out to feed at night
4. Sea urchins eat seaweed
5. The leafy sea dragon
6. The male seahorse
7. In the tentacles of sea anemones
8. No, they are living animals and aren't made from jelly
9. Yes – many such as the red soldierfish can see well in the dark
10. Special ocean parks
11. The boxer crab
12. Electric rays
13. They march to an area where they can breed or lay their eggs

index